Spring

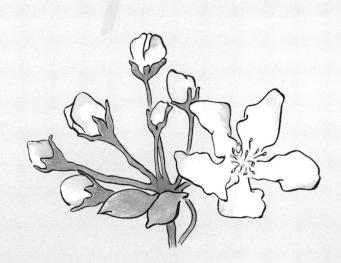

A TWELVE MONTHS RHYME

BASED ON AN OLD POEM BY GREGORY GANDER

SCHOLASTIC PRESS • NEW YORK

Copyright © 1999 by Nancy Tafuri. • All rights reserved. • Published by Scholastic Press, a division of Scholastic Inc., Publishers since 1920. Scholastic Press and colophon are trademarks and/or registered trademarks of Scholastic Inc. Text based on poem titled "The Twelve Months," by Gregory Gander (also known as George Ellis), from The Third Treasury of the Familiar, ed. Ralph L. Woods, Macmillan, 1970. The poet lived 1745-1815. ISBN 0-590-18973-5 • Library of Congress Cataloging-in-Publication Data available. • Library of Congress number: 98-47509 10 9 8 7 6 5 4 3 2 1   9/9 0/0 1 2 3 • The artwork was created with watercolors. • Book design by Marijka Kostiw Handlettering by Bernard Maisner • The text was set in Trajan Bold and Goudy. • Printed in Singapore   46 First edition, October 1999

NANCY TAFURI

Snowy
Flowy
Blowy

JANUARY

Snowy

Flowy

F E B R U A R Y

MARCH

Blowy

APRIL

Showery

Flowery

M A Y

JUNE

Bowery

Hoppy

JULY

AUGUST

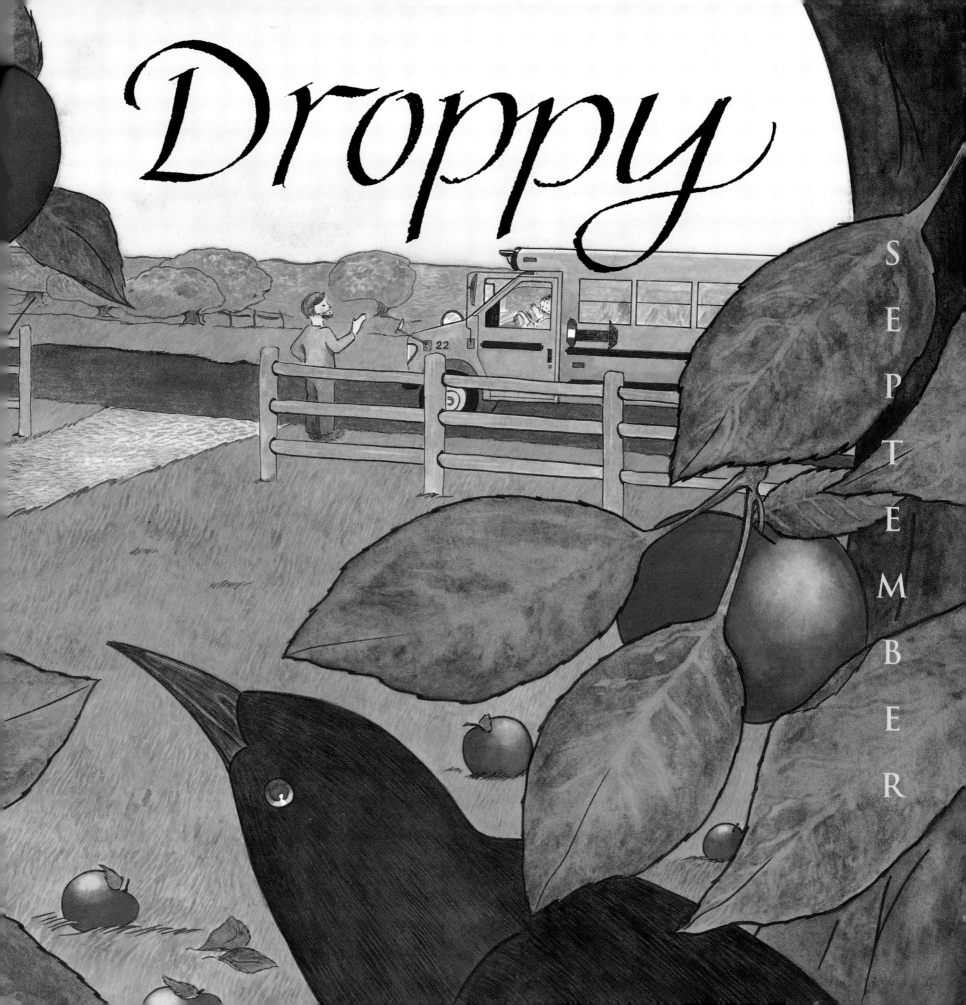

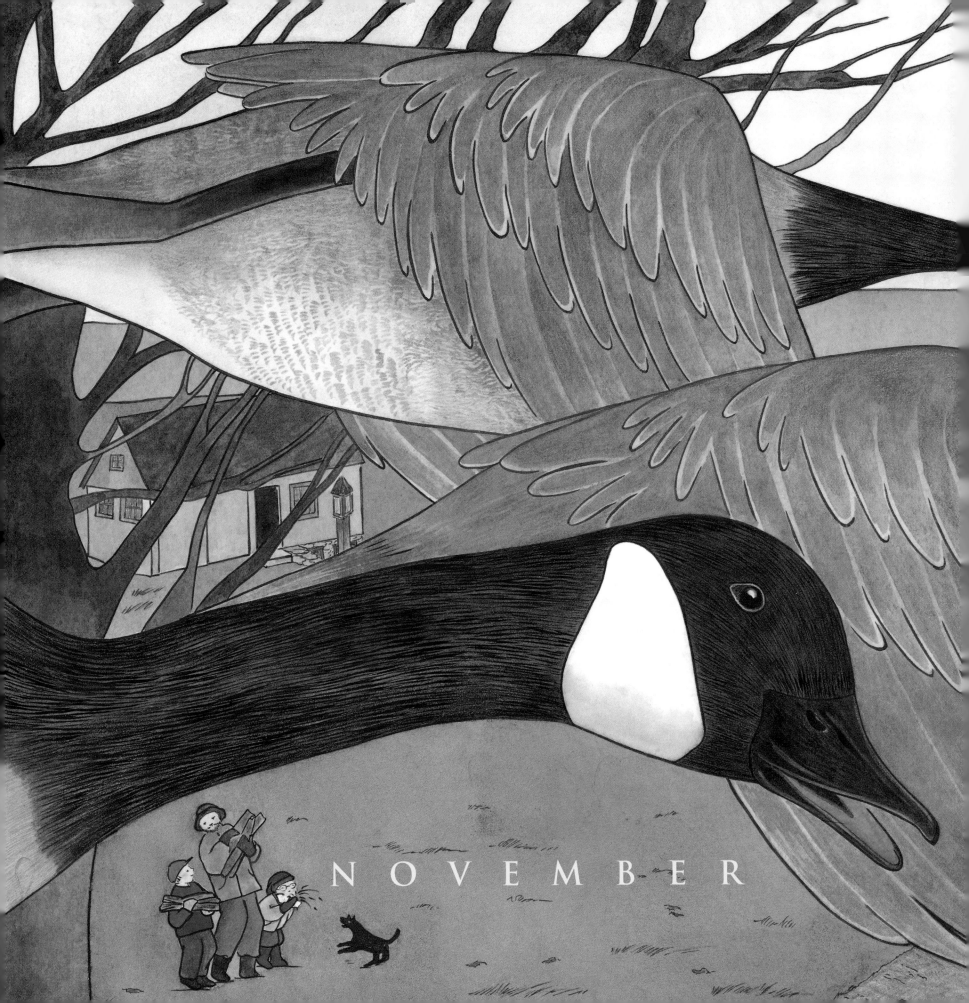

NOVEMBER

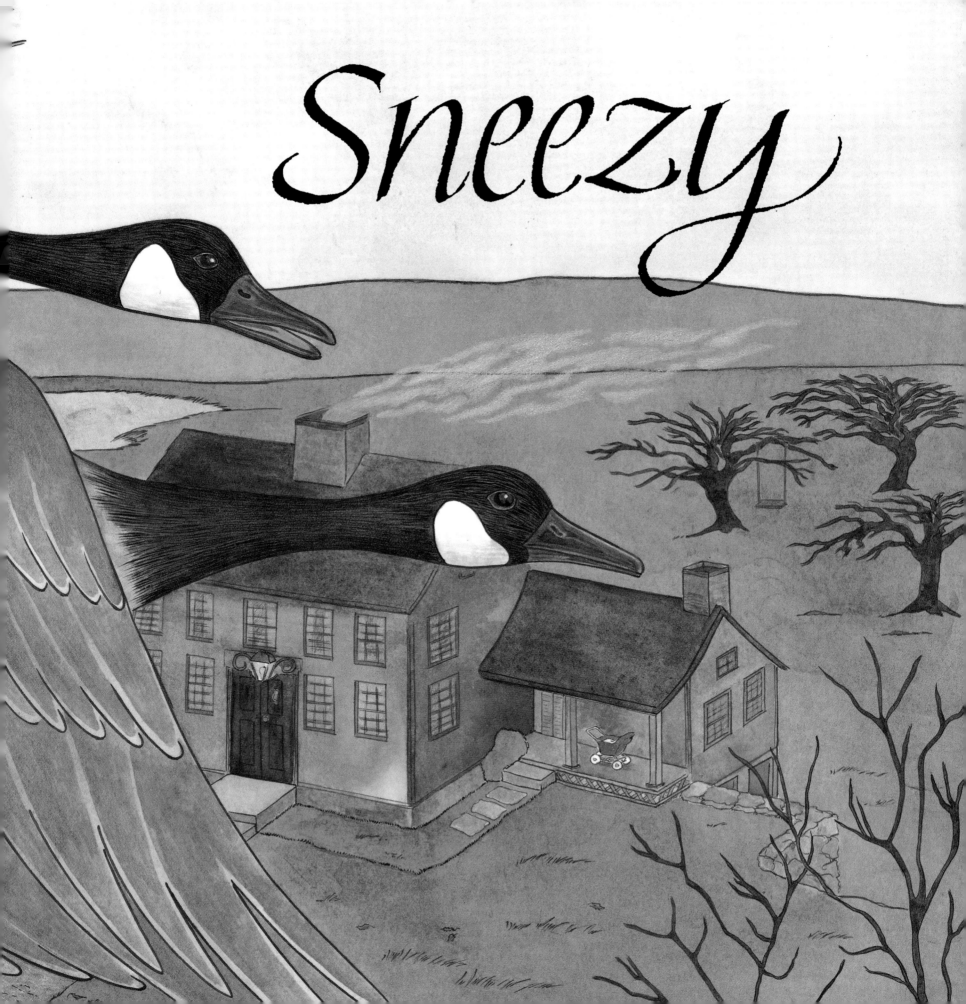

Summer